The five wives of Silverbeard

by Adela Turin,
Francesca Cantarelli and Nella Bosnia

Writers and Readers Publishing Cooperative

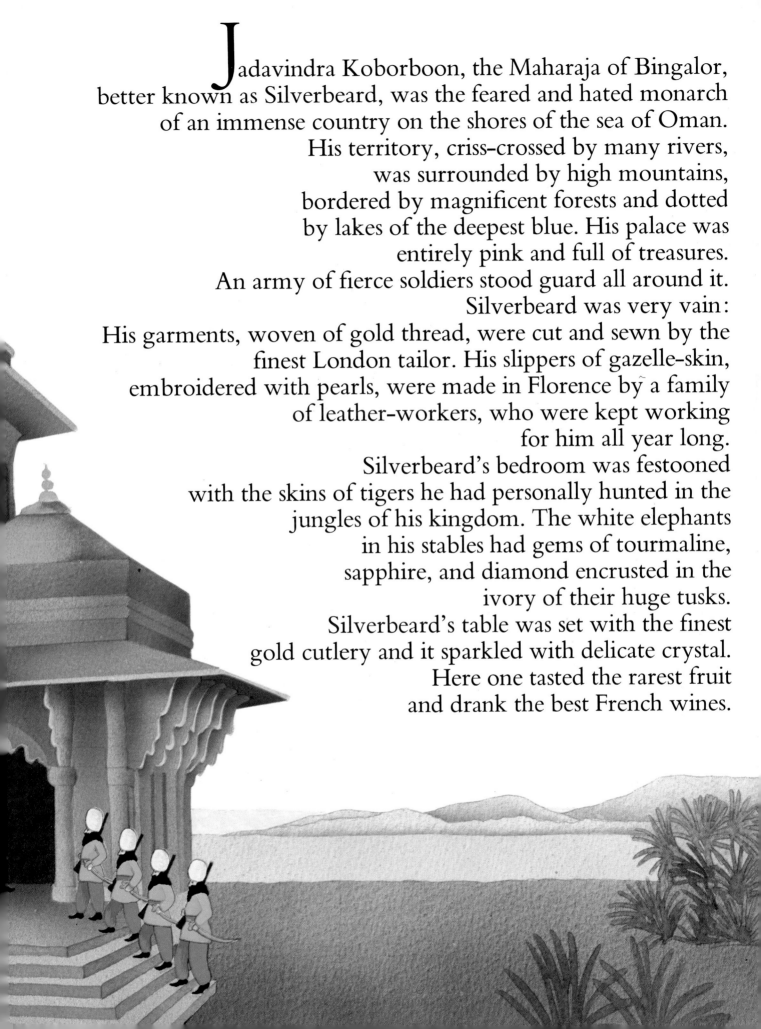

Jadavindra Koborboon, the Maharaja of Bingalor,
better known as Silverbeard, was the feared and hated monarch
of an immense country on the shores of the sea of Oman.
His territory, criss-crossed by many rivers,
was surrounded by high mountains,
bordered by magnificent forests and dotted
by lakes of the deepest blue. His palace was
entirely pink and full of treasures.
An army of fierce soldiers stood guard all around it.
Silverbeard was very vain:
His garments, woven of gold thread, were cut and sewn by the
finest London tailor. His slippers of gazelle-skin,
embroidered with pearls, were made in Florence by a family
of leather-workers, who were kept working
for him all year long.
Silverbeard's bedroom was festooned
with the skins of tigers he had personally hunted in the
jungles of his kingdom. The white elephants
in his stables had gems of tourmaline,
sapphire, and diamond encrusted in the
ivory of their huge tusks.
Silverbeard's table was set with the finest
gold cutlery and it sparkled with delicate crystal.
Here one tasted the rarest fruit
and drank the best French wines.

Reclining on his tiger skins and silk carpets, Silverbeard
would talk of the hunt and about his jewels
with other visiting princes.
From time to time, he would tour round his immense territory
in his private train which was decorated with gold filigree
and which ran over hundreds of miles of silver rails.

The peasants, who cultivated the fruit and vegetables
for his table, who extracted precious stones from his mines
and watched over his tea, cotton, pepper,
ginger, silk and resin plantations, saw him pass
and were filled with fear.
And Silverbeard contemplated his riches.

Once, having spent a particularly long and boring winter, Silverbeard thought of getting married. The moment seemed right to him and so he went to put his request to his father, Chandoola Koborboon, better known as Pot-Belly. Pot-Belly thought the matter over for a few days and suggested Lisa, one of the daughters of the Maharaja of Moneegosh. And so it was that Lisa, beautifully clothed and covered in jewels, left the palace of her father to make her way, on elephant-back to Silverbeard's pink palace. Lisa was gentle and submissive and knew neither how to read nor how to write. She was not particularly adept at the art of conversation and she said "Yes" to everything. Silverbeard threw a tantrum: "Why do you always say yes? Couldn't you say no from time to time?" "Yes, my dear," a terrified Lisa answered.

Two weeks later, at the end of his wits, Silverbeard decided to get a divorce. In order not to displease his father-in-law, the Maharaja of Moneegosh, he built a beautiful emerald-green palace, filled it with rare furniture and magnificent carpets; and there he installed Lisa and surrounded her with a legion of servants.

Lisa wept a few tears and sighed once or twice. Then she decided to raise cats and dogs and plant roses, all the while singing in a beautiful clear voice, the simple songs of her childhood.

Silverbeard went back to see his father.
He had decided to give marriage another chance.
"This time I understand" said Pot-Belly,
"what a man of your wits needs is Hannah, the poetess,
the daughter of the grand Vizir of Beekanoor. She entertains
the entire court by reciting her poems and accompanying
herself on the sitar. Hannah is intelligent and witty.
Her humorous repartee and her songs make everyone
in the court of Beekanoor laugh for months."
Silverbeard was enthusiastic:
"At last, a wife who is good company," he thought.
And so it was that Hannah,
wearing an emerald as big as a
bar of soap, arrived on elephant-back
at the pink palace.
The next day, Silverbeard had Hannah
called in order to take a stroll
round the rose garden with her.
But Hannah sent a reply
saying she could not come.
She was in the middle
of writing a song.
Silverbeard threw a terrible
tantrum, forbade her
to compose her "stupid songs",
and confiscated her sitar.

That very evening after dinner, Hannah,
deprived of her sitar but beating out a rhythm
with her rings on the crystal goblets,
told the story of Silverbeard's rage
in iambic pentameters. She imitated him so well
that the two hundred guests were
splitting their sides with laughter.
Silverbeard turned purple with indignation.
So, on that same evening, Hannah,
with her sitar and her typewriter,
was on her way to the emerald-green palace.
Lisa was thrilled to see her.
She was a little lonely in her solitary palace,
despite the dogs and cats
and roses and birds.
Hannah's imitations of Silverbeard
amused her enormously and what with laughter
and song, life in the green palace
grew very agreeable indeed.

Disappointed, Silverbeard returned
to see Pot-Belly. "I'm really not very lucky,"
he said to him. "My first wife was gentle and
affectionate, but stupid and uncommonly dull.
My second was intelligent and witty, but cruel
and sarcastic. Help me. I want to try again."
Pot-Belly was running out of ideas.
Finally he thought of Zelda, the daughter of
the Prince of Baroda, who was immensely rich.
"Zelda is not ignorant, like Lisa,
nor pretentious, like Hannah," Pot-Belly said.
"In any case, her father's wealth is enormous.
He has more diamonds and emeralds than we have."
Silverbeard asked for Zelda's hand.
Zelda, heiress to Baroda, arrived at
the pink palace in a little private plane.
She was accompanied by a Canadian secretary,
a French coiffeur,
her dogs and innumerable suitcases.

It was party evening at the palace.
Zelda arrived three hours late
and wearing jeans.
Astonished by such bad manners,
Silverbeard could only exclaim,
"Good Gracious!"
The next day while he was sipping
his morning tea, Silverbeard was amazed
to see Zelda's little plane
flying past his window.
He was informed that Zelda had just
left for the Salzburg festival:
his new wife liked music.
A month later, Zelda returned from
Salzburg just in time to leave for Paris
the next day.
When she came back a week later,
Silverbeard had made up his mind.
"I'm going to divorce her too,
by thunder!"
Before leaving for Capri,
Zelda stopped in at the green palace
to meet Lisa and Hannah.
They were both singing when she arrived.
Zelda sat down at the electric piano
and they spent a delightful evening
making music, drinking tea and chatting.
When Zelda left, she promised to return
with instruments and music,
records, books and tape-recorders,
and to stay for some time
at the emerald-green palace.

Silverbeard grew more and more depressed.
Once more, Pot-Belly was given the task of finding another wife
for his son. "Try to do better this time... I've had just
about enough!" Silverbeard said to him ill-humouredly.
Pot-Belly thought the matter over carefully
and then stated his opinion:
"What you need, since you're a man of character and strong
personality, is a simple, modest girl, who's got a head on
her shoulders. A good housekeeper, gentle and discreet.
Florinda, for example, the daughter of the groom.
What do you think?"
Silverbeard was a little doubtful, but accepted.
Florinda arrived at the pink palace on elephant-back,
as Lisa and Hannah had done before. But this time
there was no feasting and partying.
After all, Florinda was his fourth wife, and on top of that,
her relations were not particularly well-placed.

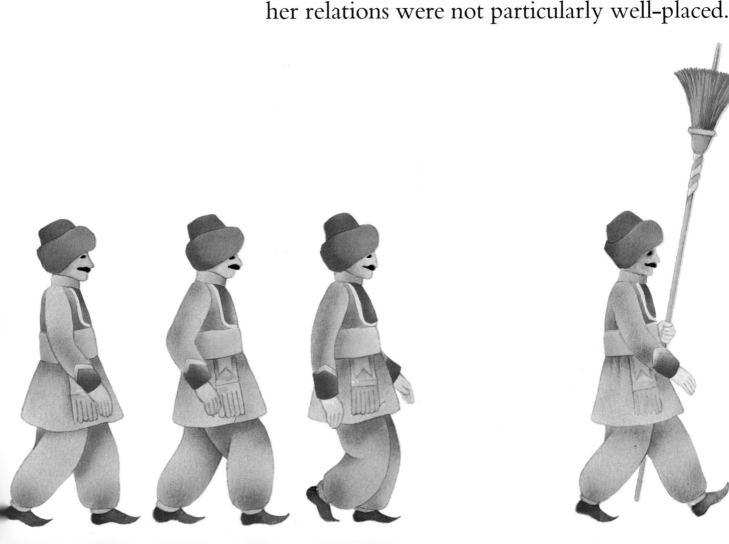

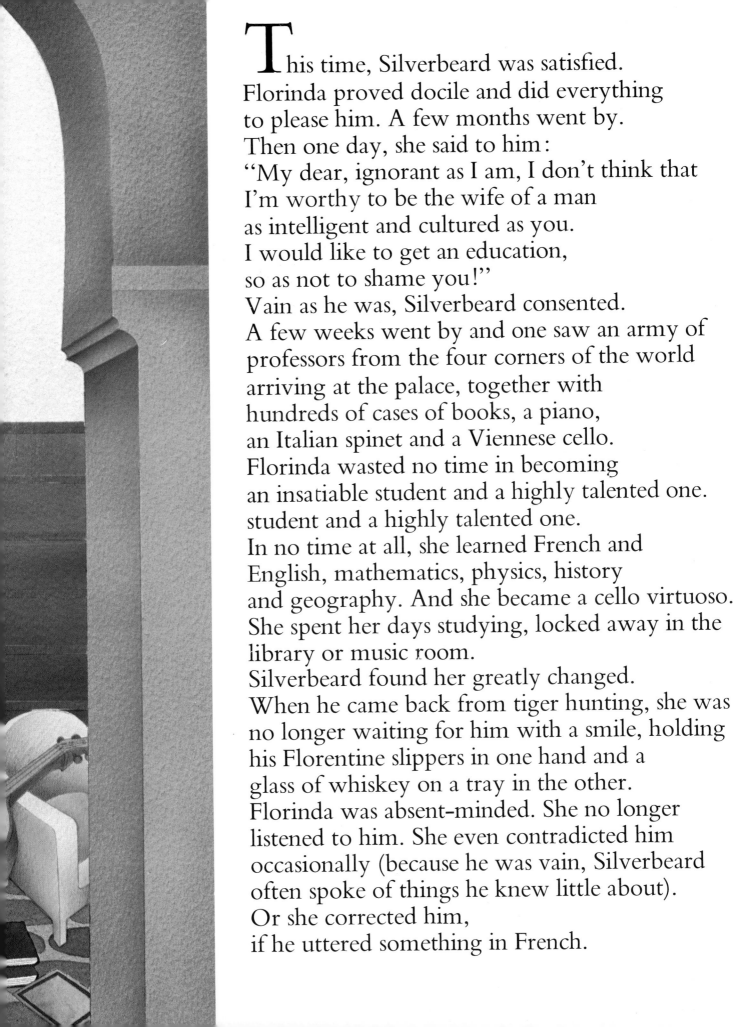

This time, Silverbeard was satisfied.
Florinda proved docile and did everything
to please him. A few months went by.
Then one day, she said to him:
"My dear, ignorant as I am, I don't think that
I'm worthy to be the wife of a man
as intelligent and cultured as you.
I would like to get an education,
so as not to shame you!"
Vain as he was, Silverbeard consented.
A few weeks went by and one saw an army of
professors from the four corners of the world
arriving at the palace, together with
hundreds of cases of books, a piano,
an Italian spinet and a Viennese cello.
Florinda wasted no time in becoming
an insatiable student and a highly talented one.
student and a highly talented one.
In no time at all, she learned French and
English, mathematics, physics, history
and geography. And she became a cello virtuoso.
She spent her days studying, locked away in the
library or music room.
Silverbeard found her greatly changed.
When he came back from tiger hunting, she was
no longer waiting for him with a smile, holding
his Florentine slippers in one hand and a
glass of whiskey on a tray in the other.
Florinda was absent-minded. She no longer
listened to him. She even contradicted him
occasionally (because he was vain, Silverbeard
often spoke of things he knew little about).
Or she corrected him,
if he uttered something in French.

Annoyed by so much learning,
humiliated by his inability to compete, and jealous,
Silverbeard decided to divorce her too.
And so it was that Florinda, deeply immersed
in a new book, took the road towards
the emerald-green palace.
Her books and her cello followed closely after.
Lisa, Hannah and Zelda – who had settled in
the green palace after her return from Capri –
welcomed her with a little uncertainty.
But they were quickly reassured.
Florinda was sympathetic and affectionate.
And she was a first-rate cellist.

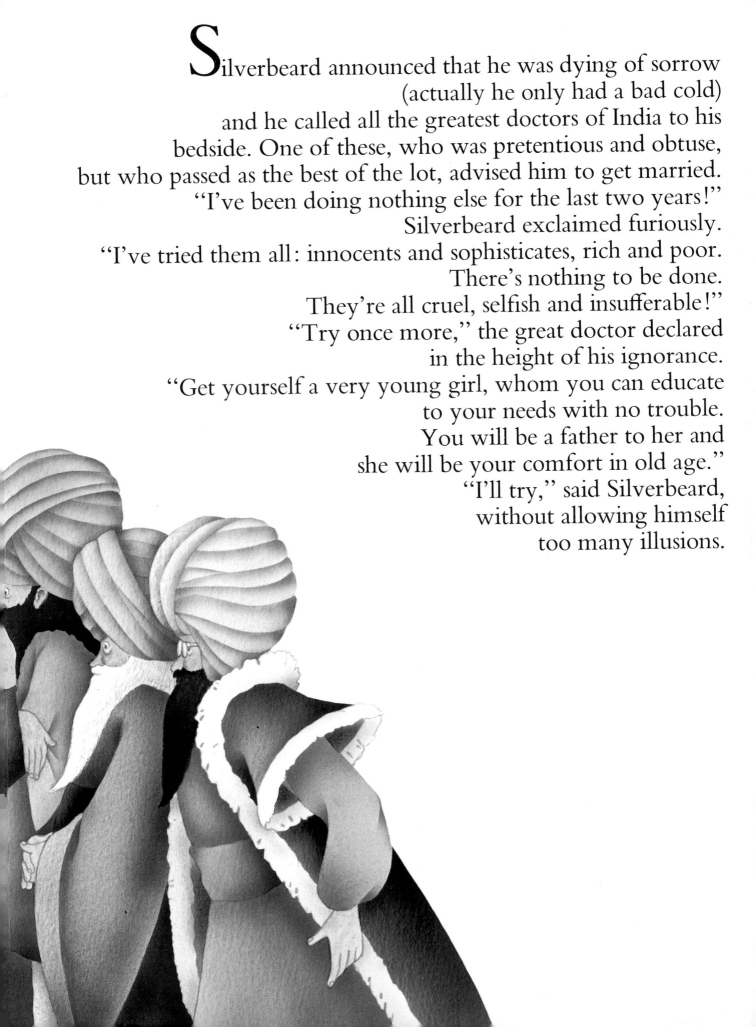

Silverbeard announced that he was dying of sorrow
(actually he only had a bad cold)
and he called all the greatest doctors of India to his
bedside. One of these, who was pretentious and obtuse,
but who passed as the best of the lot, advised him to get married.
"I've been doing nothing else for the last two years!"
Silverbeard exclaimed furiously.
"I've tried them all: innocents and sophisticates, rich and poor.
There's nothing to be done.
They're all cruel, selfish and insufferable!"
"Try once more," the great doctor declared
in the height of his ignorance.
"Get yourself a very young girl, whom you can educate
to your needs with no trouble.
You will be a father to her and
she will be your comfort in old age."
"I'll try," said Silverbeard,
without allowing himself
too many illusions.

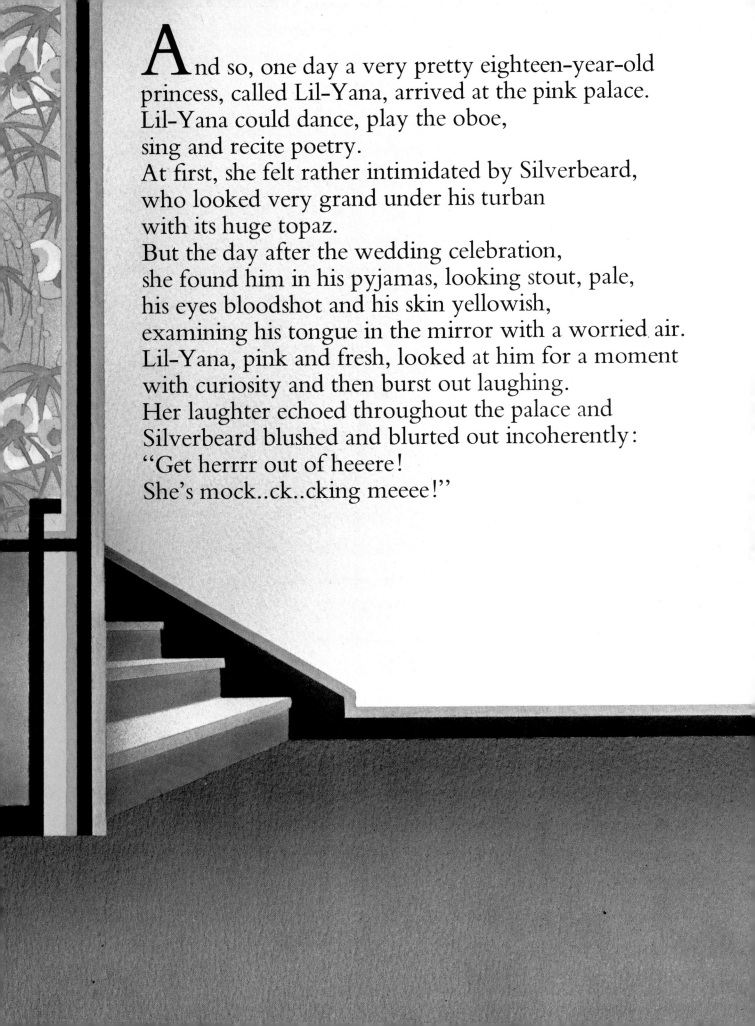

And so, one day a very pretty eighteen-year-old
princess, called Lil-Yana, arrived at the pink palace.
Lil-Yana could dance, play the oboe,
sing and recite poetry.
At first, she felt rather intimidated by Silverbeard,
who looked very grand under his turban
with its huge topaz.
But the day after the wedding celebration,
she found him in his pyjamas, looking stout, pale,
his eyes bloodshot and his skin yellowish,
examining his tongue in the mirror with a worried air.
Lil-Yana, pink and fresh, looked at him for a moment
with curiosity and then burst out laughing.
Her laughter echoed throughout the palace and
Silverbeard blushed and blurted out incoherently:
"Get herrrr out of heeere!
She's mock..ck..cking meeee!"

Two days later, Lil-Yana and her oboe
were part of the brilliant little orchestra
at the emerald-green palace.
During the summer season,
Lisa proposed that they tour the country
and put on shows on the village greens.

They had composed a comic opera in two acts,
complete with arias, recitatives, ballets
and a solo for each instrument.
It was called "Halfbeard and his Seven Wives"
and it told in burlesque fashion of the matrimonial adventures
of one Jadavindra Koborboon of Bingalor.
Wearing a false beard and a pot-belly,
Florinda imitated the Maharaja so well that,
on all the village greens where they performed,
the peasants fell about with laughter.
The opera was an immense success.
For two years, the company continued its tour of the country,
in two Mercedes-Benz caravans
that Zelda had ordered from Dusseldorf.
In all the thousand villages of Silverbeard's kingdom,
the peasants laughed until the tears ran down their cheeks.

Silverbeard's subjects, who until then had hated him –
but feared and respected him –
started to laugh at his emissaries when they came round
to collect the heavy taxes which had enriched
the Koborboon family's treasury for centuries.
Silverbeard couldn't believe his ears and boarded his
golden train on a mission to re-establish order.
But the peasants found him so grotesque since Florinda had done
her imitation of him, that they mocked him without constraint
and didn't pay a single rupee.
Now Silverbeard is ruined.
The topaz and pearls have been sold, the rugs and elephants
as well, and even the pink and emerald-green palaces.
Silverbeard lives in exile on the Riviera in a little
two-storey villa and is furious and alone.
After their grand tour of India,
Lisa, Hannah, Zelda, Florinda and Lil-Yana have performed
their shows in the biggest theatres of both east and west.
They now have a widely varied repertoire;
but "Halfbeard and his Seven Wives"
remains the public's favourite show.

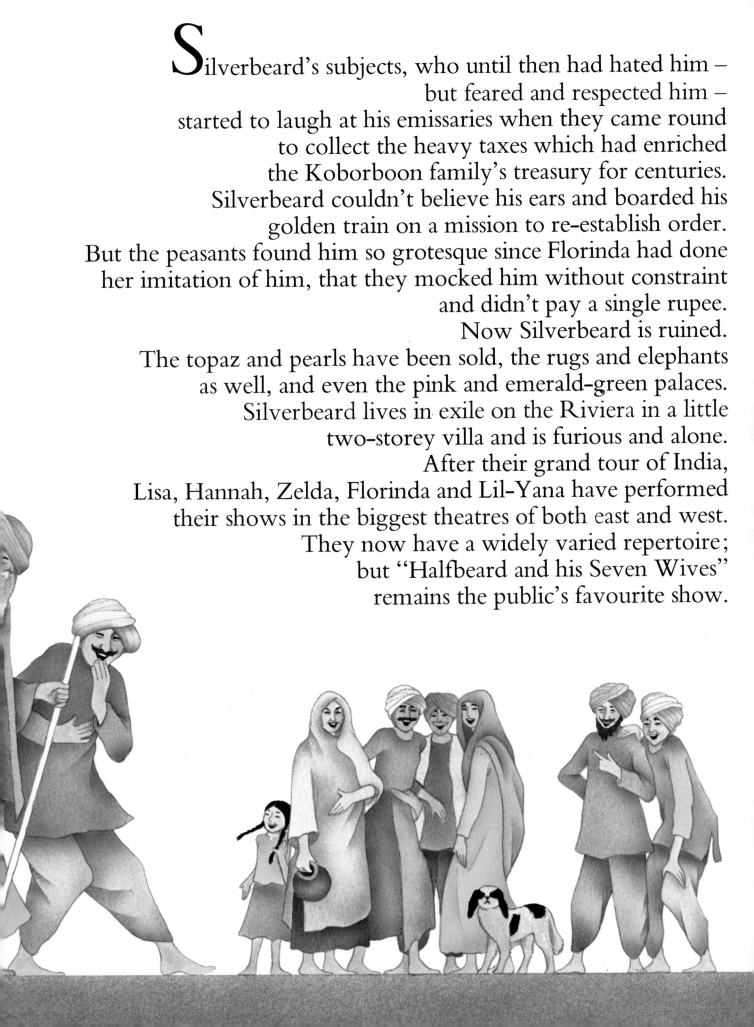